FAST & FURIOUS
SPY RACERS
SLEEPER SHIFT

by Liz Marsham
Illustrated by
Patrick Spaziante

PENGUIN YOUNG READERS LICENSES
An Imprint of Penguin Random House LLC, New York

Photo credit: cover (texture on title) KrulUA/iStock/Getty Images Plus

Fast & Furious franchise © 2020 Universal City Studios LLC.
TV Series © 2020 DreamWorks Animation LLC. All Rights Reserved.

Published by Penguin Young Readers Licenses, an imprint of
Penguin Random House LLC, New York. Printed in the USA.

Visit us online at www.penguinrandomhouse.com.

ISBN 9780593094969   10 9 8 7 6 5 4 3 2

PROLOGUE

On a beautiful Friday evening at the pier, as the sun set over the water, Tony Toretto was racing his muscle car up the roller-coaster track.

Tony screeched around the spiral leading up to the coaster's big drop-off. He saw the thief ahead of him on the tracks. In a breathtaking move, she ramped her car off the incline just before the drop, opened her driver's-side door, and flung herself out over the ocean.

"This is gonna be bad," Cisco's dismayed voice said in his ear.

Tony careened out of the spiral and toward the incline. "I can reach her," he said. "My suit—"

Cisco cut him off. *"But your suit won't—"*

"I know," responded Tony. "Frostee, can—"

"Yeah," said Frostee, *"but it still—"*

1

"*I got you,*" Echo Pearl cried. "*Cisco, come on!*"

Tony nodded. *My crew,* he thought. *Best in the world.*

"*Toretto, what are you* DOING???" screamed Ms. Nowhere.

Tony let out a low chuckle. "Respecting the rules," he said. He thumbed the button on his steering wheel to fire his rocket boosters, and the muscle car bucked under him, shooting forward. He barreled up the incline and held his breath as his tires left the track. With his car now above the ocean, Tony hung suspended and weightless. He unbuckled his seat belt, opened the door . . . and stepped out into nothing.

CHAPTER 1

"It is time to start respecting the rules!" declared Ms. Nowhere. She paced up and down the garage, scowling at Tony and his friends as they lounged around the TV.

A *clank* from across the warehouse-like space drew Tony's attention, and he looked over with a grin. Ms. Nowhere's staff had been busy all morning reinstalling the last of the team's upgraded equipment. Before they started spying for Ms. Nowhere and her secret branch of the government, Tony and his crew—gearhead Cisco, artist Echo, and hacker Frostee—had been scrounging for car parts at the dump. Now Tony watched as Gary, Nowhere's assistant, flipped a breaker next to a giant Yoka Spirit Water mascot head. With a whir, the Yoka head began to light up and blink as, one by one, the screens

3

embedded in it came to life.

"Aaaaaaall right!" cheered Frostee. He dropped the video game controller he was holding and unfolded himself from his cross-legged position on the table. With a flourish, he rolled his shoulders and cracked his knuckles. "The hub is back online. I am gonna do so much hacking!"

"And *I* am gonna do so much *snacking*!" said Cisco from the couch, staring impatiently at the nacho dispenser. "Just as soon as that cheese warms up."

Next to Cisco, Echo chuckled. "It's not gonna heat up any faster with you watching it, you know."

Cisco raised one eyebrow dubiously. "You sure about that?" He leaned forward and rubbed his hands together hungrily, narrowing his eyes at the machine. "I don't know if I wanna take that chance."

Echo scooped the controller off the table, then settled into the cushions. "Pretty sure, bro." She patted Cisco on his giant back. "But you do you."

"No! Do not do you!" snapped Ms. Nowhere. She stomped over to stand by the TV. "That is entirely the problem. *Gary!*"

Gary fished a complicated-looking remote out of his pocket, pointed it at the TV, and pushed a button. On the screen, the fighting game disappeared, replaced with blank nothingness.

Echo opened her mouth to protest, but shut it again when Ms. Nowhere turned an icy glare on her.

"As I was saying . . ." Ms. Nowhere locked eyes with Tony, then Frostee. She looked toward Cisco and cleared her throat pointedly. "Eyes front, big guy."

Cisco let out a small whimper. "But, nachos . . ."

"I took your cheese away once," hissed Ms. Nowhere. "I can do it again."

Cisco's eyes snapped to her. "You wouldn't," he whispered.

"Wouldn't I?" Ms. Nowhere held Cisco's gaze for a long moment, until he gulped audibly. Then she nodded, satisfied. "As I was *saying*, it is time—*past* time—for you all to start respecting the *rules*." Keeping her eyes locked on Cisco, she pointed at the TV screen.

Tony lifted a hand. "Uh, which rules?"

"These—" Ms. Nowhere started, then glanced at the TV. "Ugh. *GARY!*"

Gary winced, then pushed another button on the remote. The words THE RULES appeared across the top of the screen in stark black type.

"You managed to capture Shashi and the Skeleton Key, yes," Ms. Nowhere said. "But that operation was entirely too sloppy. If you're going to work for me, you need to learn some discipline. Not every problem can be solved by driving a car at it."

"Hey, we do more than that!" Tony protested.

"Do you?" challenged Ms. Nowhere. "Do you *really*?"

"Yeah," said Echo. "Sometimes we drive cars *away* from things."

"Or off them," said Frostee with a laugh.

"Or through them!" Cisco put in.

"You are making my point for me,"

Ms. Nowhere said with a sigh. "I understand, you're seventeen—well, except for you, kid." She nodded toward Frostee, who crossed his arms grumpily and muttered under his breath. Tony made out the words *almost* and *fourteen*.

"Most teenagers aren't known for their discipline," continued Ms. Nowhere. "But most teenagers don't have secret government jobs where they risk their lives, and most teenagers don't answer to me. So for this next mission, you are going to learn to focus more on the 'spy' and less on the 'racer.' Gary!"

Gary gestured with the remote, and *Rule #1: Stick to the plan* appeared on the TV.

"No more wild, last-minute ideas, people," Ms. Nowhere said. "I will give you a plan, and you will carry out that plan. Got it?" Before any of them could respond, she snapped, "Next!"

Another line of text popped up. *Rule #2: Trust your resources.*

"Along with the cars and the video games and the nacho cheese, I have provided you

with top-of-the-line spycraft here," Ms. Nowhere said, waving her arms to indicate everything in the garage. "You obviously enjoy it. Tony, if I'm not mistaken, you're wearing your new wingsuit under your clothes right now, even though we are nowhere near an airplane."

Tony blushed. "It's comfy."

"It is," agreed Ms. Nowhere. "So when you are tempted to go off plan and improvise at the first sign of trouble, instead, think: how can I use what I have to follow rule number one?"

"But what if—?" Tony started.

Ms. Nowhere cut him off with a *"Next!"* She stabbed a finger at a new, bright red line of text on the TV: *Rule #3: Follow orders.* "If there is *any* question about what you should be doing, you will ask me, I will tell you what to do, and you will *do it.* Now let's put the rules into practice. *Next!"*

The rules disappeared, replaced by a list of company names that Tony only vaguely recognized.

"For the last three nights," Ms. Nowhere went on, "security firms downtown have been hacked and their data stolen. One firm each night. These firms have an extensive client roster—*next!*"

The company names disappeared, replaced by a much longer list. Tony scanned it quickly, seeing banks, tech companies, even some government departments. He heard Echo draw in a breath.

Ms. Nowhere nodded solemnly. "With the information the hacker has stolen, they could be planning on breaking into any—or all—of these computer networks. Millions of people's private information is at risk. But here's the good part: each of the hacks has begun on the firm's local network. In other words, the thief is actually *in* the building at the time. And here's the *best* part." She leaned toward the team. "I already know who she is." She waited a beat, then two. Nothing happened. "Oh, for the love of— Gary, take a cue! NEXT!"

"Sorry, sorry," Gary murmured, and the text on the TV was replaced with a CCTV still of an older woman. Her light gray hair framed her face, contrasting with her dark-brown skin and black clothes. She stared directly into the camera, as if daring it to take her picture.

"This is Alecto," announced Ms. Nowhere. "We've been after her for a long time. Together, she and her two partners were known as the Furies, after the Greek goddesses of vengeance. They made their hacking careers targeting companies that behaved badly but managed to dodge criminal charges. In their own eyes, the Furies were vigilante heroes. They were meticulous and they were careful, but not careful enough. We caught Megaera and Tisiphone a few years ago, and since then Alecto has gotten sloppier." Nowhere shook her head at the picture on-screen. "She never would have let herself be filmed like this in the old days. She's bolder now that she's on her own . . . and possibly more dangerous. Gary, the binder!"

Ms. Nowhere planted one hand on her hip and pointed at the TV with the other. "That is your target, team. And this"—she swiveled her finger to point at Gary, who dumped a thick binder on the table with a *thunk*—"is your plan. And what is rule number one? Toretto?"

Tony rubbed a hand across his face. There were a lot of pages in that binder. "Stick to the plan," he answered grimly. He flipped open the cover and saw schematics for an office building downtown. *At least I'll get to drive my sweet spy car over there*, he thought.

CHAPTER 2

"Come on," Tony complained from the bed of Cisco's truck, "can you drive this thing any faster?"

"Nah, Tony," replied Cisco. "Ms. Nowhere said speed limit all the way this time." He turned a corner, being careful to signal first, and pointed at the building ahead of them. "Besides, we're there."

As Cisco drove past, Tony and Echo raised their heads cautiously from where they were hunkered down in the truck bed. What they saw was . . . well, if Tony was being completely honest, what they saw was boring. The square, glass-enclosed office building took up the entire block. Here and there throughout the building, a light shone in an empty office, most likely where someone had forgotten to turn it off. On the ground floor, Tony could see through the floor-to-ceiling windows into a spacious lobby, lit only by dim security lights. The streets were deserted except for a beat-up sedan parked opposite the front door.

In the passenger seat, Frostee slipped on his VR headset and held up his backpack. Four pods detached from the outside of the bag and unfurled into small flying robots. As the drones shot out the open passenger window, they shimmered and became transparent. "Ghost drones away," Frostee said. "Fly, my spooky friends, fly!"

Cisco drove the truck to the middle of the next block and parked. He twisted in his seat, nodding at the lone sedan. "I'll keep lookout from there," he said. "But if anything happens, just call and I'll—"

"If anything happens," came Ms. Nowhere's voice over their earpieces, *"you'll what now?"*

Cisco startled. "Uh, I'll—I'll stick to the plan," he answered.

"Which is?"

"To keep watch unless you say otherwise."

"That's right."

The four of them got out of the truck and crept quietly toward the building. Tony saw the frown on Cisco's face and chucked him on the shoulder. "We'll be fine, don't worry," he said. "And if the old lady brought a crew, and we walk into a fight, we'll make sure to chase them out of the building first so you can help."

Tony, Echo, and Frostee left Cisco hunkered down by the sedan and quickly crossed the street. They hid behind a decorative shrub outside the main entrance while Frostee's cloaked drones buzzed around the building, scanning for security guards through the lobby windows.

"Okay," Frostee said a moment later, watching the readout in his goggles. "Looks like just one guy, and he's awake. Alecto must have snuck by him."

"Whoa," came Cisco's voice in their earpieces.

"Oh, come on, it's one dude!" snorted Echo. "Sneaking by one dude is not that impressive."

"No, not that," Cisco whispered. *"It's this car."*

"What, the sedan?" asked Tony.

"Yeah," breathed Cisco. *"The wheel is . . . huh."*

"What about the wheel?"

"Let's keep the chatter down!" interrupted Ms. Nowhere. *"No one cares about the hunk of junk you're using as cover."*

"That's the thing, though," said Cisco. *"It looks like a hunk of junk, but I swear this wheel is custom. And that dash has way too many switches to be—"*

"Cisco," hissed Ms. Nowhere. *"You have one job as lookout, and that is to look! Out!"*

"I am," Cisco insisted. *"I'm telling you, something is weird about this car!"*

"The guard is up and moving," Frostee said from beside Tony. "I think he's gonna go take a leak."

"Team, this is your window," said Ms. Nowhere. *"Get that forged access card ready, and remember, it's the second—"*

"Second bank of elevators on the right, we know," Echo said, rolling her eyes.

"Maybe I should pop the hood," muttered Cisco.

17

Tony heard shuffling over the earpiece and risked a glance across the street. In the dim light, he saw Cisco crouched in front of the sedan, tapping his chin thoughtfully.

"Hey," whispered Cisco, *"remember that story Mitch was telling us a couple of days ago? About the stolen cars?"*

"Cisco," said Ms. Nowhere. *"I am ordering you to forget about the car! And what is rule number three?"*

Cisco opened his mouth to answer . . . and then he recoiled, half-standing as the sedan's engine roared to life.

"What the—?" Frostee exclaimed, pushing his goggles down and turning to look.

"CISCO!" barked Ms. Nowhere.

"I didn't do it!" cried Cisco. *"It must be controlled remotely!"*

"Cisco," Tony said urgently, "get away from that car!"

But in the next instant, the sedan, with no one at the wheel, shifted into gear and shot forward. With a *whoof,* Cisco doubled over and was popped up onto the hood. He had

just enough time to jam his fingers between
the windshield and the hood before, with a
screech, the car peeled around the corner and
out of sight.

CHAPTER 3

"Frostee," Tony yelled, "get the drones after him!"

"You got it, T," replied Frostee. He frowned behind his VR headset, and Tony heard whirring around him as the ghost drones broke off their recon and whizzed away.

"Let's go!" Tony grabbed one of Frostee's arms to guide him while he controlled the drones. Echo grabbed Frostee's other arm, and the three of them began sprinting for Cisco's truck.

"What are you doing?" Ms. Nowhere protested in their earpieces. *"Our people just picked up a data download coming from the firm. The hack is happening right now. Get in there!"*

"Are you kidding?" Echo said, disbelieving. "That car stole Cisco!"

"Rule number one! Cisco can handle himself, and the way you described that beater, it's not going anywhere fast."

"It's a sleeper!" Cisco yelled through the comm. His voice was strained and almost drowned out by rushing wind and engine noise.

"Cisco, you okay, man?" Frostee said, climbing into the truck's passenger seat. "The ghost drones should catch up to you any second now."

"It's a sleeper!" Cisco repeated.

"He's right," said Tony, starting the truck as Echo swung into the bed. "Did you hear that engine tone?"

"I heard it," Echo said. "I think the truck can take it, though."

Tony gunned the engine and peeled away from the curb. "Why is a self-driving sleeper parked in the middle of a deserted block downtown?"

"A self-driving what?" asked Ms. Nowhere. *"No, wait, I forgot: I DON'T CARE. Get back to the mission right now!"*

"Take this left!" Frostee yelled.

"Hold on, Echo!" Tony called, and he jerked the wheel hard. The truck screeched around the corner, and Tony upshifted and leaned into the gas pedal.

"Don't worry about me, worry about catching that sleeper!" Echo yelled back.

"Right!" Frostee ordered. "Then the northbound highway ramp on your left. The drones have him in sight!"

As Tony careened onto the highway, he heard Ms. Nowhere take a deep, exasperated breath. *Someone needs to start talking to me. Right. Now,* she said, her voice icy cold.

"A sleeper is a car that looks normal on the outside, or even beat-up," explained Tony, cutting over to the left lane and pouring on speed. "But under the hood, it's a different story. Top-of-the-line engine, turbocharge, you name it."

Gary's voice cut in on the comms. *"What's the point of that?"*

"Gary," chastised Ms. Nowhere, *"you're encouraging them again!"*

"It's interesting, though," Gary said softly.

"Take the 2!" called Frostee, and Tony wove around merging cars, skidding onto the berm as he rocketed up the on-ramp to the new highway.

Echo raised her voice to be heard over the rush of wind. "In a race, the sleeper is supposed to mess with your head. You think you're racing a broken-down old sedan, right up until it leaves you in the dust."

"That trick—whoa!—only works once, though," Cisco grunted, the effort of holding on clear in his voice. *"Once you know the racer, it doesn't matter—aaaaah!—what the car looks like."*

"Cisco, stop talking and hold on!" scolded Echo.

"No, keep talking," Frostee said. "My drones weren't made for racing speeds; they can't keep up with you. Where are you going?"

"We just turned onto the—yaaaaah!— Angeles Crest!"

Tony looked up just in time to see the sign for Angeles Crest Highway flash by, the arrows pointing to the two right lanes.

"Plenty of time," he muttered, shooting a glance in the rearview mirror and cutting the wheel hard to the right. Amid blaring horns, the truck blasted across three lanes, narrowly making the on-ramp.

"We must be right on his tail!" Echo shouted. "Can you see him?"

Now on residential streets, the highway quickly narrowed to one lane in each direction, then wound up into the mountains.

Ms. Nowhere's voice came again, thin with impatience. *"You know, Tony, there are other—"*

"There he is!" Tony called. The sedan, headlights off, was expertly drifting around the hairpin turns ahead as the road climbed higher and higher. Tony could just make out Cisco's flailing form clinging to the hood.

A long sigh came through the earpiece. *"Have at it, then,"* Ms. Nowhere said.

"These tight turns—oof!—are not—aaah!—easy, you guys!" With a jolt, Tony realized that Cisco was starting to sound tired. *"It's gonna shake me!"*

Tony glanced to the right. Inches past the guardrail, a sheer cliff dropped off into blackness. If Cisco lost his hold on one of these turns . . .

"No, Cisco!" came Echo's voice. "Try to break through the windshield!"

"But what if—"

"Try it now, Cisco!" called Frostee. "I'm looking at the GPS, and the next hairpin isn't for half a mile!"

"AAAAAH!" Cisco bellowed, psyching himself up. Tony heard a *crack*, then *"OW. That's not gonna work."*

"Maybe use your feet?" shouted Echo. "One good kick!"

"Oh boy," muttered Cisco, and then Tony heard *"GRRRRRAHHH!"* followed by a *thwack*.

"Hold on, here comes the turn," Tony said. "We're right behind you!"

The sedan's tires screamed as the car drifted to the left around the hairpin. Cisco screamed louder, but he managed to hang on. Tony cut the wheel and downshifted, and the truck screeched after the car. Tony gritted his teeth and braced against the force pulling him to the right, then the rear of the truck *ping*ed off the guardrail, just as he came out of the turn and upshifted again.

"That was close, Tony," Echo said. "I don't have Cisco's iron grip back here."

"Sorry, Echo," replied Tony. "I can catch him before the next one."

"This glass must be reinforced," Cisco cried. *"I can't even—WHOA!"*

A cone of brightness lit up the front half of the sedan. Cisco squirmed and blinked in the sudden light.

"That's a drone!" cried Frostee. Squinting at the top of the cone, Tony saw that he was right: a large, sleek drone was pacing the sedan, propellers whirring.

"It's trying to make him lose his grip," yelled Echo. "Look!"

As she spoke, the drone went into a dive. Cisco yelped and dodged as the drone clanked off the hood, just inches from his head.

"We've gotta move fast," said Tony. "Everyone hold on."

Echo, Frostee, and Cisco yelled back in unison, *"We ARE!"*

Tony floored the gas and twisted the wheel, and the truck crossed into the oncoming lane, pulling up on the sedan's left.

"Cisco, jump!" shouted Echo.

Cisco shifted his weight, preparing to leap. But the drone swooped down and dove again, and he was forced to shrink back against the hood. *"This thing's like a guard dog!"* Cisco yelled.

"I got you!" said Frostee, holding his backpack out the window. "Sic 'im, backpack drone!"

Rotors sprouted from the corners of Frostee's backpack and began to spin, and the bag lifted out of Frostee's hand and into the air. It bobbed and darted around the guard drone, blocking its path to Cisco.

Frostee held out his hand.

When it was clear, Echo yelled, "Now, Cisco!"

Ahead of them, Tony saw headlights. "Hurry!" he shouted. "There's another car coming!"

With a roar, Cisco gathered himself and jumped across the gap. He wrapped both hands around the truck frame, and Echo grabbed his belt to steady him. "I'm on!" he shouted.

Tony slammed on the brakes and dodged behind the sedan. A minivan swept by in the lane where the truck had been a moment before, horn honking wildly. A second later, the strange drone shot across the road in front of them, momentarily blinding Tony with its light.

"Aw, lug nuts, my eyes!" Tony yelled, throwing up his arm.

"The sleeper!" Echo called, just as Frostee said, "The drone!"

When Tony dropped his arm, he saw the flash of brake lights from the sedan and slammed on his own brakes instinctively. The truck fishtailed on the narrow road as the sleeper executed a neat skid into a small lookout parking lot that opened off to the right. By the time Tony wrestled the truck under control and brought it to a stop in the lot, the sleeper had rocked to a halt and turned itself off.

"Man, I lost it!" Frostee cried, throwing his hands up in frustration. He jumped out of the truck and held up his arms, and a few seconds later the backpack drone lowered itself onto his back and folded away its rotors. "That drone headed straight up over the mountain, and once it turned off its light, I couldn't find it."

Tony, Echo, and Cisco jumped down from the truck, and the four of them approached the car together. The only sound was the ticking of the car's engine as it cooled. They looked at one another, confused. What had just happened?

"In case anyone was wondering about, you know, THE MISSION," Ms. Nowhere's voice suddenly blared in their ears, making them jump, *"the hack is complete, and Alecto will be long gone. I have to admit, I thought you would*

at least break the rules one at a time instead of tossing them all out at once!"

"This can't be a coincidence," said Tony. "It's too weird. The theft has to be connected to this car somehow."

"Did you ever consider that the car was a decoy, meant to lure you away?"

"Maybe," said Cisco dubiously, "but then, what was with that drone?"

"It showed up once you started messing with this thing," Echo said, giving the sedan a light kick. "Like it was protecting something. What if . . ." She trailed off, getting down on her back on the asphalt and scooting under the car.

"What are you looking for?" Tony asked.

"Anything that—gotcha!" Echo slid out and held up a flat square with rounded edges, as big as her palm.

"That is *not* what I think it is," breathed Frostee, snatching the square. Tony heard a series of beeps as Frostee's VR goggles ran a diagnostic, and then Frostee nodded. "That is *exactly* what I think it is. It's a transmitter!"

A second later he gasped and pointed to the car. "This is the hack, right here! Alecto was using the car as a router so she could break in remotely!"

"So that means . . ." Cisco trailed off.

"It means," Tony finished, "Alecto was never anywhere near that building."

CHAPTER 4

"Gary, bring up the rules again," said Ms. Nowhere, shaking her head. "Go wide."

Gary tapped the remote, and the lines of text appeared on every screen in the garage, including the team's phones. Tony heard a grunt of frustration from the Yoka hub, where Frostee was busy examining Alecto's transmitter. Frostee looked over his shoulder, narrowed his eyes, then started typing furiously. One by one, the screens in the hub cleared, and Tony smiled. *I have a feeling Gary's remote is about to turn into a very fancy paperweight*, he thought.

Tony and Ms. Nowhere had been arguing for over an hour, pacing around the boxing ring, and they were getting . . . well, nowhere. One by one, his friends had drifted away from the conversation. Frostee was working on the transmitter. Echo had climbed up the car lift and was working on spraying an elaborate tag high on the wall. Cisco was working his way through a giant pile of nachos. Even Gary was darting glances at the arcade cabinet next to the couch. But Tony couldn't let it go. He *knew* he and his crew had done the right thing.

"Having a job means having a *boss*, Tony," Ms. Nowhere said.

"But you know exactly who you hired," Tony countered. "And you know we would never leave family in danger."

"Rule number two: Trust your resources!" snapped Ms. Nowhere. "In this case, me! Did it occur to you that my people could have easily tracked that sedan and intercepted Cisco?"

Tony rocked back on his heels. "Uh, no," he admitted.

"Gary's not just here for his skills with the remote, you know," Ms. Nowhere said.

"Do you have *Leethal Legendz* on this thing?" Gary murmured to Cisco, motioning to the cabinet with his chin.

Cisco nodded enthusiastically. "You know we do! The original and all five sequels!"

Gary hummed in appreciation. "I was a beast on *LL3* back in the day."

"What?" Cisco shoved a handful of chips in his mouth and dusted off his hands. "I goh-uh shee thish," he said through the food, rising to his feet.

"Gentlemen," Ms. Nowhere said icily. Gary and Cisco froze in place, then guiltily lowered themselves onto the couch.

"Look," said Tony. "Gary could have tracked Cisco, but could he have driven like we did to save him? Could any of your people?"

Gary shook his head. "Not quite like you did, no," he said.

"And if we hadn't been there when the sleeper stopped, we wouldn't have found the transmitter, and we wouldn't know how the thefts are happening. We're getting the job done!"

"You're getting *lucky*," countered Ms. Nowhere.

"The bottom line is," said Tony, "if you're

going to make plans for us, the plans have to include us having each other's backs."

Ms. Nowhere crossed her arms. "Then you're going to hate this next plan, because I've narrowed Alecto's next target down to two places, and you're going to have to split up."

"But what about the transmitter?" Tony asked. "Maybe that could help?"

Frostee leaned out of the hub. "Bad news, T," he said. "The way this thing works, I can trace its signal while it's transmitting, but once it cuts out, it's gone. And I won't even be able to track it unless we're in range. So once the hack starts, we gotta get to where the signal's coming from fast."

Tony started to grin at the word *fast,* but Ms. Nowhere raised a finger.

"All the more reason to split up," she said. "We don't know where this thing will start *or* end, and if this is our only lead, we need you covering as much distance as possible."

"Hold on," Echo chimed in. "This isn't our only lead." She swung down from the car lift and turned to Cisco. "Right before you got car-napped, you brought up that story we heard from Mitch."

Cisco's face lit up. "That's right! He had a couple of buddies with high-end sleeper cars that got stolen, one after the other."

"Yup," Echo nodded. "The cars were taken in the morning and found the next day in some random place with their electronics shot. The dudes were trying to figure out who was punking them, thought maybe it was us."

"Who's got time for that?" Tony snorted.

Cisco shrugged. "Us, a year ago. Except, you know, more 'surprise tagging of the new paint job' and less 'straight-up theft.'"

"Good point." Tony turned to Echo. "So you think maybe Alecto is using the same trick every time, turning the sleepers into routers?"

"It's worth checking out," said Echo. "Frostee—"

"I've been hacking since you said 'stolen,'" Frostee replied distractedly. Tony turned to see Frostee typing busily, data flying across the screens in the hub. "I've got the GPS histories for Mitch's buddies here. They spend most of their time driving between garages and taco stands, but look at this." He pointed to a few lines in the first log. "Ms. Nowhere, where's the place that got broken into on Monday night?"

"Tenth and Grand," Ms. Nowhere said.

Frostee nodded. "The first car spent, like, six hours parked on that block before it drove to Griffith Park and fried itself. What about Tuesday?" He squinted at the second GPS log. "Lemme guess, is it on Wilshire near Figueroa?"

There was a pause, and Tony looked over at Ms. Nowhere. "Is that . . . do you look *impressed*?" he asked.

Quickly, Ms. Nowhere shook her head. "Hardly. Now we know where Alecto has been, but we already knew that. We still don't know where she's going."

Tony held up his phone. "Rule number two," he said. "There's a huge resource we haven't used yet: Layla. If anyone will know the most likely sleeper car to be taken next, it's her." He brought up Layla's number, discreetly smoothed his hair, and hit send on a video chat request.

Echo rolled her eyes. "Tony, you've been texting her for weeks. No answer. What makes you think she's gonna—?"

"Tony?" Layla's face popped up on his phone. "You're calling me, it must be important. What's up?"

"Hi!" Tony blurted, then got ahold of himself. "I mean, hey, how's it going? Where are you?"

Layla leaned closer to the screen, her ponytail swinging onto her shoulder. Tony couldn't see around her head; she could have been next door or on the moon, for all he knew. "What's up, Tony?" she repeated. "I only have a minute."

"Oh, uh. Right. Have you heard anything about sleeper cars in LA getting jacked?"

"Yeah, I did. It's up to four now, right? Why?"

"Long story, but if you were going to take, like, the next best sleeper in the city, which would you pick?"

"Oooh, good question. Tino's been working on one for years, looks like a pickup, but it's actually all ultralight carbon fiber with a rocket under the hood. But there's also that girl Jezz. Hers looks like one of those teeny little cars that can barely break forty, but *woo*, y'all should see that thing go."

Tony heard the rattle of keys as Frostee started to search. He nodded at the screen. "Thanks, Layla. When you're around, we should—"

"Gotta go, Tony." Layla smiled and broke the connection.

"Bye, Layla," Tony muttered. He looked up and saw Echo smirking at him. "What? She answered, didn't she?"

"It's Tino's pickup," Frostee declared. He hit a button, and a screen filled with a police report. "Reported stolen an hour ago. I'm tracking it now . . . looks like it's in . . . Woodland Hills?"

"One of the firms on my list is in a corporate park in Woodland Hills," Ms. Nowhere said. "That must be the next target."

"And Alecto will be holed up somewhere nearby," Tony said. "This is great. As soon as she starts the hack, we've got her!"

CHAPTER 5

"Frostee, do you have her yet?!" Tony shouted. He upshifted and passed a convertible on a narrow corner.

The hack had started much earlier than the others, and now Tony, Echo, and Cisco were chasing the converted pickup down Topanga Canyon Boulevard. Frostee, in the passenger seat of Cisco's pickup, was doing his best to find the signal's origin.

"This lady is tricky," Frostee complained over Tony's earpiece. *"I can't pin her down!"*

"We're almost out of road," called Echo. *"When we hit the coast, do we turn north or south?"*

"A few minutes ago, I would have said she was north," grumbled Frostee, *"but now ..."*

Ahead of them, the pickup blasted through the light and turned right, heading north.

47

"*Remember the rules,*" said Ms. Nowhere over their comms. "*Gary!*"

The displays in Tony's and Echo's cars flickered, then showed Ms. Nowhere's "The Rules" image . . . except now the text at the top read "YOKA Rules!" alongside a grinning Yoka head. Tony and Echo chuckled.

"*What did you do to Gary's remote?!*" Ms. Nowhere demanded.

"*Improved it,*" said Frostee gleefully.

"Aw, man," Gary said.

Ms. Nowhere cleared her throat. "*As I was saying. The plan is for you to catch* her, *not her router. The pickup could be a distraction.*"

"*South, the signal is definitely south!*" Frostee cried.

Tony wrestled with the wheel, threading through traffic without losing speed and turning left onto the Pacific Coast Highway. "This would have been easier in the middle of the night," he muttered. "So many tourists!" He checked his side mirror. Echo and Cisco were right behind him.

"*Tony, look out!*" Echo shouted.

Tony snapped his eyes to the front. The guard drone from the previous night was diving right toward him!

"AAAAAH!" he screamed, downshifting and twisting the wheel. The muscle car slewed into the oncoming lanes, narrowly missing the drone. Tony quickly regained control and upshifted as Echo and Cisco shot by him. He swerved back to the southbound lanes and took up position behind them.

"Where'd it go?" he called.

"I'm right here," a staticky voice said from right beside his ear.

"AAAAH!" he screamed again. The drone was pacing his car just outside his open window.

"You're a screamer," the voice observed.

"You can hear me?" Tony sputtered.

"And a thinker," the voice added.

"Is the drone talking to you?" Cisco asked.

Tony opened his mouth to respond but waited as a plane passed low overhead on its way to the airport. When the noise of its engine had subsided, he yelled, "It's Alecto!"

"Definitely a thinker," said the voice dryly.

"Keep her talking!" ordered Frostee. *"I can use the drone's broadcast frequency to help track her! Arrgh, she must be using relays to bounce . . ."* His voice got softer as he muttered to himself.

"Why are you doing this?" Tony shouted out the window. He figured that was as good a conversation starter as any.

"Why are *you* doing this?" Alecto countered. "Trying to stop me?" A loud, staticky roar came from the drone's speaker, drowning Alecto out for a moment. Then she continued, *"I'm* doing this for *you!"*

"You're what now?"

"You and your friends are just kids! You deserve to grow up in a world where shady corporations are forced to play by the same rules as everyone else. My friends and I worked for that our whole lives, and I'm so close. Back off, and I can finish my life's work and give you this gift!"

Echo's sleek electric car dropped back to pace the drone on the other side. Tony saw her listening intently through her open window.

"If you use what you've stolen," Tony argued, "it'll expose private details about a lot of innocent people. The people who use those banks and stuff don't deserve to be punished."

"Justice always comes at a price," Alecto told him.

Tony shook his head. "Your price is too high."

A laugh came from the drone's speaker, followed by a rising whining noise. Tony looked over quizzically. Were those sirens?

"You sound just like my old crew," Alecto said. "Always wanting to play it safe. And what happened to them? *They* got caught, and *I* didn't. I'm better off on my own. No one can let me down this way."

"Tony, look left," Echo said. Tony cut his eyes over, past the drone, and saw a knot of fire trucks pulling to a stop around an accident in the far lane, their sirens winding down. *"The sirens. The plane engine. We heard them through the drone."*

"The signal is moving!" Frostee shouted

suddenly. *"That's why I can't pin it down!"*

"She's driving on this road!" replied Echo.

"She must be right in front of us!" Tony added.

"Rule number two, Tony," said Ms. Nowhere. *"We can clear the roads for you and set up a roadblock. Just make it to the pier."*

Tony grinned and floored the accelerator. He could make it anywhere with his crew, never mind the few miles to the pier. And with the sun just starting to set over the ocean, it was a great evening for a race. "We're on it, boss," he said.

"Well, then," said Alecto. "Time to make this interesting."

CHAPTER 6

Ahead of them, Tony saw a sudden commotion on the road. A boxy yellow car cut across oncoming traffic, smashed through the guardrail, and drove straight up the embankment that ran to their left.

"Change of plans, Ms. Nowhere!" shouted Tony. "Alecto's headed for Ocean Park!"

"Copy," said Ms. Nowhere tersely. Tony heard her muttering as she gave orders to her people in the background.

"That is no ordinary hatchback," Cisco said appreciatively. *"It took that hill like whoa."*

"She must have stolen another sleeper," said Tony.

"Still the thinker, I see," came Alecto's voice through the drone. "But no. This one's mine. Bye, kids."

The roar of a rocket engine came through the drone's speaker as a burst of flame shot from the hatchback's tailpipe, and the sleeper rocketed into the park, smashing the fence that ran along the top of the hill. The drone lifted away from Tony's car and took off after the hatchback.

"She's in the park!" shouted Tony.

Ms. Nowhere spoke rapidly in his ear. *"Here's the plan: Frostee, keep tabs on that drone. Tony, you stay on Alecto. If you can, herd her away from town and onto the beach; that's the safest place for a confrontation at this time of day. Echo and Cisco, peel off onto the beach and pace Tony from there. My people are setting up a roadblock just south of the pier and managing the civilians. If she insists on staying close to the crowds, we'll pen her in there. GO!"*

"Already gone," Tony said, and pushed the button on his steering wheel for the rocket boosters. The car leaped forward. He gauged the oncoming traffic, expertly spotting his window, and twitched the wheel to the left. The muscle car shot through the narrow gap in traffic and through the hole Alecto had made in the guardrail. Tony felt the tires sink into the loosely packed earth of the hillside and begin to spin out. He tapped a button on his display, and a grappling hook shot from the front of the car, catching on the fence. He reeled in the line, and the car tilted up at a forty-five-degree angle as it climbed the hill, tires catching on firmer ground. The rocket boost was almost gone. Tony released the hook and pushed the gas pedal all the way to the floor, and the muscle car shot over the top of the hill, catching air. A second later, the car landed in Ocean Park with a *crunch*.

Tony quickly took in the scene. To his left, people stood along the asphalt paths of the park or sat in the grass, frozen, staring at him. To the right was chaos. A vendor cart was tipped over. People were lying flat in the grass, having thrown themselves to safety, and the cable fence that bordered the path was smashed flat. Tony shifted into gear and took off to the right.

He spotted her right away. The boxy car was weaving from the path to the grass and back again, dodging pedestrians and benches, smashing into trash cans as it hurtled south. "I see her!" he cried. "She's headed straight for the pier."

"*Roadblock's in place, Tony. We're evacuating the last of the civilians as I speak,*" replied Ms. Nowhere. "*Stick to the plan, and whatever you do,* do not lose her. *That is an order. Echo and Cisco, are you in position?*"

"*We're on the beach,*" came Echo's voice, "*but we feel like we're missing the fun up there.*"

"I'll try to bring the fun to you," Tony said with a grin, and gunned the engine. Just ahead, Alecto swerved to the right to avoid a large decorative cannon set into a wide part of the path. Tony upshifted, screeched around the cannon to the left, and tried to cut her off. At the last possible moment, though, she fired her rocket engine again and shot by him.

Tony swore under his breath and brought his car around after her. He was running out of room to get Alecto onto the beach: the pier

was coming up fast on the right, and straight ahead he saw a tight line of sleek black cars stretched across the path, curving around to the left to block escape on that side.

"What is she doing?" he muttered. Alecto seemed to be headed straight for the roadblock. "Look out, she's gonna ram it!" he yelped.

But just as he cried out, Alecto's car went into a skid, drifted gracefully around to the right, and took off down the deserted pier.

"We've got her!" Ms. Nowhere crowed.

Tony frowned. "Where is she going?"

"There's nowhere to go!" said Ms. Nowhere. *"It's over!"*

Tony shook his head. "Not yet," he said, and wrenched his wheel to the right. The muscle car took the corner at speed, and Tony headed down the empty pier after Alecto.

The wide concrete bridge arced down to a series of shops and restaurants on either side, and soon Tony's car was bouncing over wooden slats where the pier jutted out over the water. He glanced to the right and saw Echo's and Cisco's cars speeding in his direction across the beach below, their tires spraying arcs of sand. The wooden path narrowed as deserted vendor carts pressed in on both sides. Ahead of him, he saw Alecto's hatchback screech around the corner to the left, heading into the amusement park.

"She's headed for the rides!" Tony called.

"Good. She can have one last thrill before we arrest her," Ms. Nowhere said.

"Tony, what do you think she's up to?" Echo asked.

"I have no idea," Tony admitted, taking the corner into the fair. He saw the hatchback thread its way past the game booths, headed for the bigger rides behind them. The park had clearly been abandoned in a hurry: the pirate ship ride, which usually held thirty people on its huge covered boat as it swung back and forth in a wide arc, was still swinging with no one aboard, and above it he saw an empty car shoot by on the roller coaster that ringed the park. "But I know it's something—whoa!"

Alecto had just accelerated sharply. As Tony watched, agape, she crashed through a flimsy pedestrian barrier, sped up the ramp that formed the line for the ship ride, and shot off the ramp . . . right onto the swinging fake wood canopy of the ship. She gunned the engine as the ship swung to the right. Her car sailed off the end of the thin slab, caught air, and then *ka-TANG!* With a howl of rubber and metal, the hatchback landed on the roller-coaster track and began to drive along it.

"Has she lost her mind?" came Ms. Nowhere's voice.

Tony eased off the gas for a second, letting the ship complete a swing to the left. As it did, his eyes tracked Alecto's car, following the orange tracks around in a tight arc. As the hatchback came zooming around, passing along the tracks over his head, he saw Alecto in person for the first time. She looked out the window and locked eyes with him. In her gaze, Tony saw stubbornness, pride, and desperation. And then she was gone, climbing the track in a tight spiral at the landward end of the park.

"She knows exactly what she's doing. Whatever it is." Tony focused on the ship, which was beginning a swing to the right again, and took a deep breath. "Well," he said, "I guess this is happening now."

He floored the accelerator, and his car bore down on the ship ride, up the ramp, and through the air. As soon as the front tires touched the canopy, he spun the wheel to the right, aligning the car with the length of the ride. He gave the car more gas, and at the top of the ship's swing the car hurtled up, out, and toward the coaster.

CRUNCH! Tony winced as the muscle car's front corner collided with the metal tracks. He twisted the wheel to line up the back end before the car lost traction and fell from the ride. The car rocked alarmingly for an instant, then settled, and Tony breathed a sigh of relief as he accelerated.

As he bent around the arc on the far side of the park, he craned his neck to find Alecto. Her car had just come out of the spiral and was pointed toward the ocean, speeding up an incline into a steep drop.

"Toretto, I know you do not like to be outdriven," said Ms. Nowhere, *"but may I remind you that roller coasters go in a circle? You are chasing your own tail here, and for what? What's your plan?"*

"I don't know," Tony muttered.

"Drone coming in high from the north!" shouted Frostee.

Tony, headed for the spiral, looked to the right. He saw the drone banking in to hover over the water near the coaster's drop. At that same instant, he heard a *FWOOM* as Alecto hit her rockets again, and the car streaked up the incline toward the drop. Then he saw the driver's-side door open.

Suddenly he understood. "Echo, Cisco, get under the pier to the north side. *NOW!*" he cried.

The hatchback popped up off the incline

and sailed out over the ocean. Alecto threw herself from the car and grabbed the drone, wrapping her arms around its sleek body.

"*Toretto, report!*" demanded Ms. Nowhere.

"She's using the drone to get past the roadblock," Tony replied, turning into the spiral.

"*She can ride it down into the city, steal a car from there, and disappear,*" added Echo. "*Unless . . . oh no, Tony, look!*"

Tony screeched around the spiral leading up to the coaster's big drop-off and saw that the drone was bobbing erratically in the air, with Alecto struggling to control it. "It's not strong enough to carry her," he realized. "She's going to fall!" He took the last loop of the spiral, losing sight of her again momentarily.

"*This is gonna be bad,*" Cisco's dismayed voice said in his ear.

Tony careened out of the spiral and toward the incline. Time seemed to slow as Tony flashed on Ms. Nowhere's lectures from the last two days: *Stick to the plan. Tony, you stay on Alecto. Trust your resources.* And finally:

Do not lose her. That is an order.

"I can reach her," Tony said. "My suit—"

Cisco cut him off. *"But your suit won't—"*

"I know," responded Tony. "Frostee, can—"

"Yeah," said Frostee, *"but it still—"*

"I got you," Echo Pearl cried. *"Cisco, come on!"*

Tony nodded. *My crew,* he thought. *Best in the world.*

"Toretto, what are you DOING???*"* screamed Ms. Nowhere.

Tony let out a low chuckle. "Respecting the rules," he said. He thumbed the button on his steering wheel to fire up the rocket boosters, and the muscle car bucked under him, shooting forward. He barreled up the incline and held his breath as his tires left the track. With his car now above the ocean, Tony hung suspended and weightless. He unbuckled his seat belt, opened the door . . . and stepped out into nothing.

CHAPTER 7

Falling through the air, Tony clawed out of his shirt and dove toward Alecto and the struggling drone. He held out his arms and let the air catch the flaps of his wingsuit, hearing a *whoosh* as his momentum slowed.

"Alecto!" he called over the rush of wind. Alecto's head turned up and her eyes widened in surprise. Tony held out his hand as he closed the distance, using his suit to maneuver to one side of her. She shoved the drone away from her and used the momentum to close the gap between them, throwing her arms around him.

Tony wrapped an arm around her, and with the flap on that side of his suit closed, they immediately began to plummet toward the ocean. He looked wildly over his shoulder toward the beach . . . and Frostee's drone backpack, right on time, swooshed

70

up to meet him. Tony hooked his free arm through the strap and once again felt his momentum slow.

But the drone backpack was meant to carry Frostee, not Tony plus another person. Right away, the drone began to struggle and dip. They were falling again, more slowly, but not slowly enough.

Alecto snorted as the ocean came closer. "*This* was your plan, kid? What's the point? You should have just let me fall."

Tony shook his head. "That price is too high. And besides," he said, "my crew never lets me down."

The roar of a motor reached his ears, and he grinned at the sight below him. A large Jet Ski was chopping across the waves toward them at top speed, Echo at the wheel and Cisco on the back. The backpack banked toward the Jet Ski, and Tony raised his gaze to see Frostee, standing on the beach and piloting the drone, give him a thumbs-up.

The drone wavered and gave out one last high whine of its rotors. Tony and Alecto slowed just before they hit the water. Cisco reached out and snagged them from the air, pinning Alecto's arms to her side. Tony swung around behind him, and Echo turned the now-very-crowded Jet Ski back to the beach.

A fleet of black cars met them as they stepped onto the sand. A half-dozen large men in suits spilled out of the cars, jogged forward, and surrounded Alecto.

Alecto held out her hands to be cuffed and shook her head. "Should have given you more credit, kid," she told Tony ruefully. "You *are* a thinker." As the men steered her toward one of the cars, she looked at Tony, Echo, Cisco, and Frostee in turn. "You make a good crew," she said. "Never take that for granted."

"You don't gotta tell us, lady," laughed Echo.

The rear doors of the nearest car opened, and Ms. Nowhere and Gary got out. "You picked quite a time to start following the rules, Tony," she said wryly. "How did you know she had another trick up her sleeve?"

Tony shrugged, grinning. "What can I say? I'm a spy!"

"A *spyyyyyy racer!*" Frostee sang.

"Yes, well," said Ms. Nowhere, "there was rather more racing on this mission than I had anticipated. But, in the end, you all handled yourselves well. Even if you did ruin a very expensive car." She nodded toward the backpack drone in Tony's hand, now sparking and wheezing. "And a fairly expensive drone."

"And, you know," Gary said hesitantly, patting his pocket, "my remote."

"That's not ruined," said Frostee. "You know I wouldn't do you like that, man! I told you, it's *improved*. Hit up, up, down, down, left, right, left, right for me."

Gary fussed with the remote briefly. Inside the black car, a familiar video game soundtrack drifted from the dashboard screen, and Gary's face lit up. "Is that *Leethal Legendz 3?*"

Frostee nodded. "On any government-owned screen you want. You're welcome."

Gary dove back into the car, and the sounds of electronic punching and kicking began. "Oh!" he shouted after a moment. "Thank you!"

"I'll see you all tomorrow morning," said Ms. Nowhere. "I've got a surveillance job for you. But I'm sure you'll find a way to drive a car at it."

"It's what we do best," Echo said.

"And we are the best at what we do," added Cisco.

As the fleet of cars drove away, leaving the four friends on the beach, Tony, Echo, Cisco, and Frostee climbed up onto Cisco's truck and got comfortable. Cisco waved down a vendor and bought every hot dog in his cart.

Waves crashed. The sun set. Tony had risked his life today, but now he was full and happy, surrounded by his crew, his family. *Rule number one*, he thought. *Stick together. Rule number two: Trust your family. Rule number three: Follow your heart.* Now those were some rules he would always respect.